SARAH LEAN's fascination with animals began when she was aged eight and a stray cat walked in the back door and decided to adopt her. As a child she wanted to be a writer and used to dictate stories to her mother, but it wasn't until she bought a laptop of her own several years ago that she decided to type them herself. She loves her garden, art, calligraphy and spending time outdoors. She lives in Dorset and shares the space around her desk with her dogs, Harry and Coco.

Also by Sarah Lean

The Tiger Days series in reading order:

The Secret Cat

The Midnight Foxes

The Riverbank Otter

Duckling Days

For older readers:

A Dog Called Homeless

A Horse for Angel

The Forever Whale

Jack Pepper

Hero

Harry and Hope

Duckling Days

SARAH LEAN

Illustrations by Anna Currey

HarperCollins *Children's Books*

First published in Great Britain by HarperCollins *Children's Books* in 2018
HarperCollins *Children's Books* is a division of HarperCollins*Publishers* Ltd,
1 London Bridge Street, London, SE1 9GF

The HarperCollins website address is: www.harpercollins.co.uk

1

ISBN 978-00-0-816577-2

Printed and bound in England by CPI Group (UK) Ltd, Croydon CR0 4YY

For Hazel and Lolly

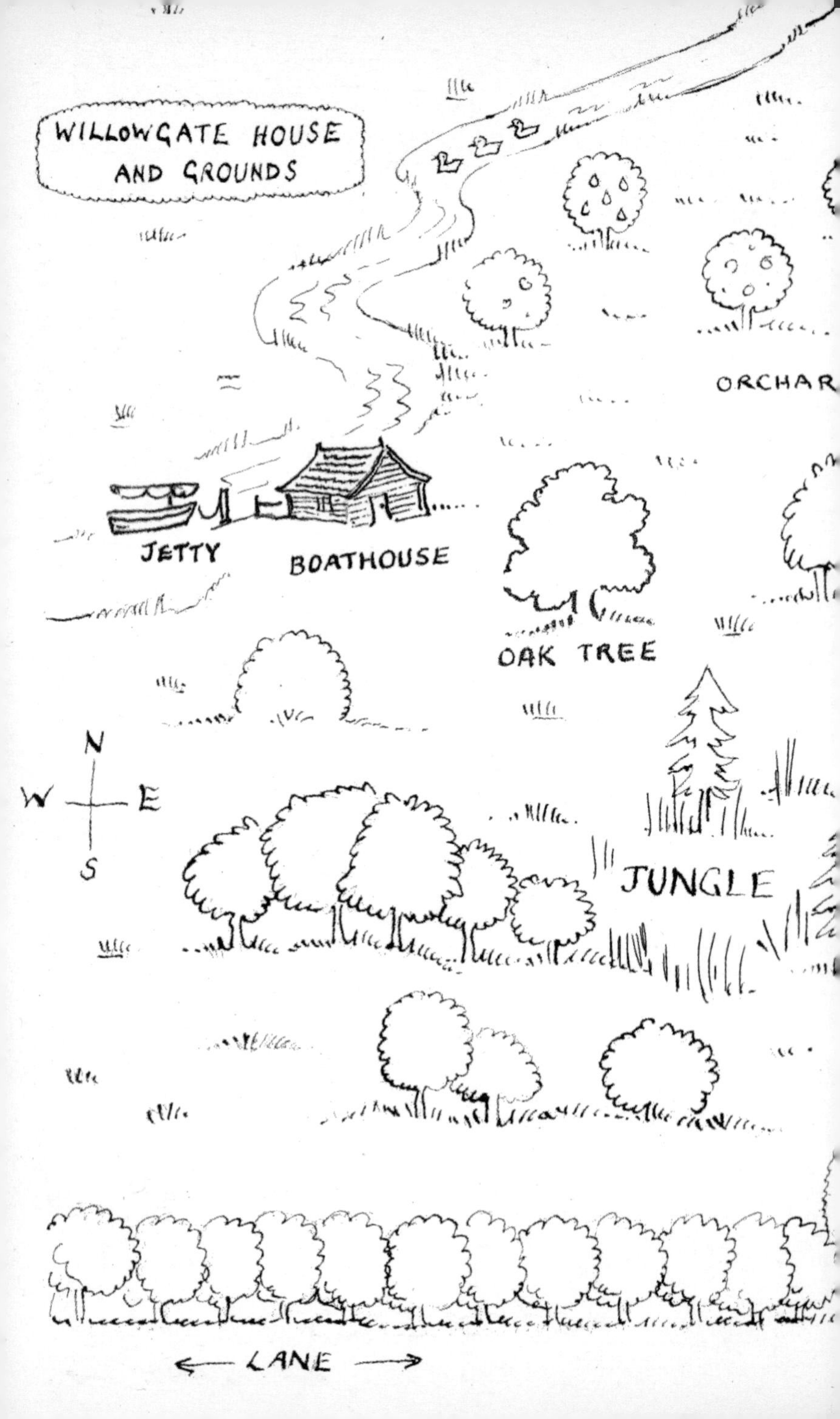
WILLOWGATE HOUSE AND GROUNDS
ORCHAR
JETTY
BOATHOUSE
OAK TREE
N
W
E
S
JUNGLE
LANE

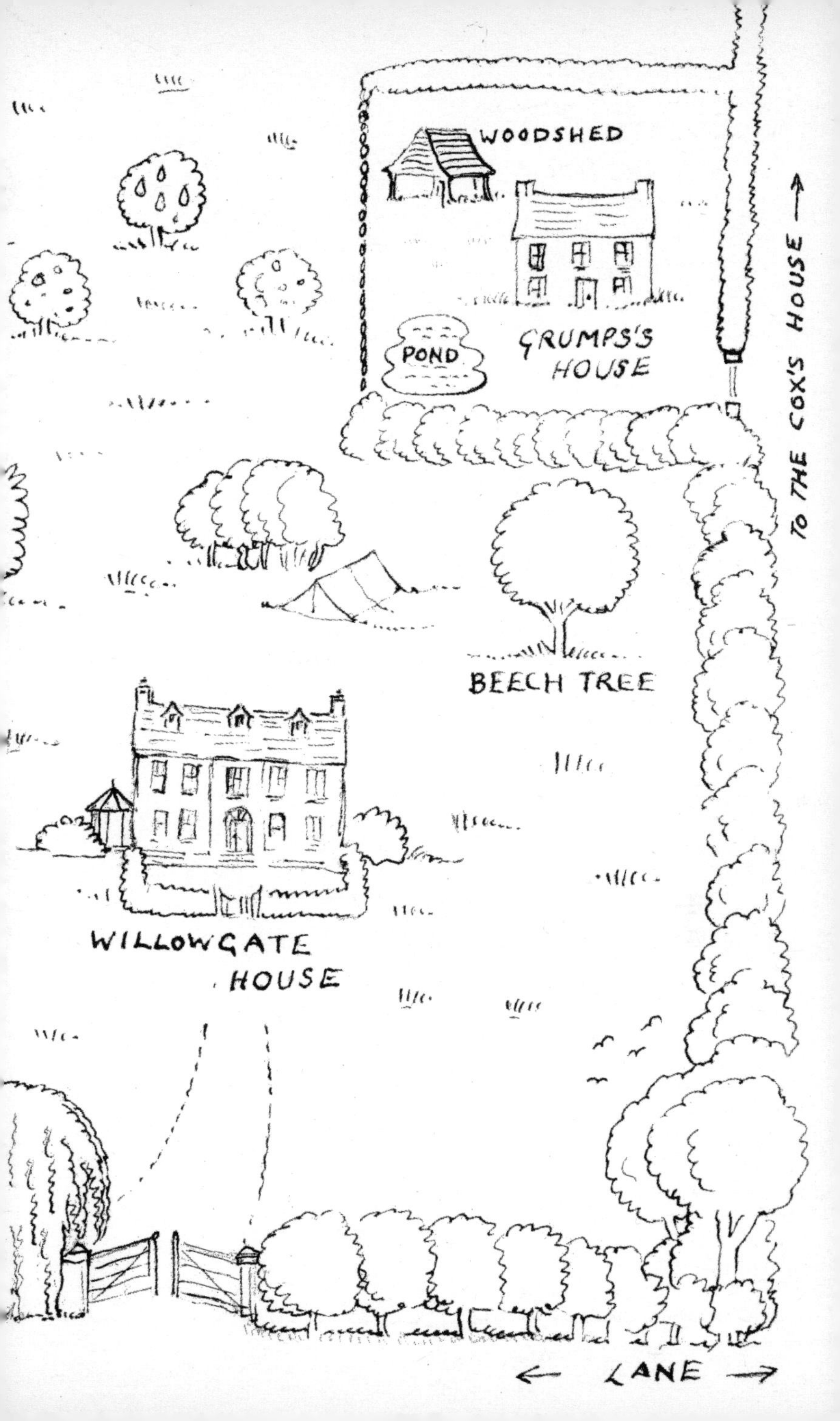
WOODSHED
POND
GRUMPS'S HOUSE
TO THE COX'S HOUSE
BEECH TREE
WILLOWGATE HOUSE
LANE

Chapter 1

A Room of Her Own

It was spring, and Tiger Days was visiting her grandmother, May Days, for the school holidays. May Days used to live in Africa, and Tiger had met her for the first time a year ago when she moved back to England to live at Willowgate House. Since then, Tiger loved staying with her grandmother, exploring the great gardens and wildlife, and becoming more and more adventurous each time. Tiger had

made friends with a boy called Tom and his grandfather, Grumps, who lived next door. She was disappointed to discover that this time they were away on holiday at the seaside, but she was looking forward to having May Days and Holly the cat all to herself.

While Willowgate House was being fixed up, Tiger and May Days had slept in the garden in a tent. Over winter, rather than move into one of the finished bedrooms, May Days had simply pitched the tent inside the big kitchen, and she was still sleeping there now.

Tiger, Holly and May Days spent their first day together wandering the gardens

to see what wildlife they could find. Birds were in the sky, fish were in the river, squirrels leapt between budding trees and a hedgehog shuffled in the undergrowth.

Tiger and her grandmother were full of wonder, chatting about what they had seen while they grilled sausages for tea on a campfire under the willow tree. They had gone to bed full and contented, listening to an owl hooting and bats squeaking through the open kitchen window.

"Nobody would know so many things live in the garden unless they looked and listened like we do," said Tiger.

"The garden is always full of life," said May Days, yawning. "And your grandmother is full of tiredness. Time for sleep. Night, night." And she turned out the lamp.

The next morning, Tiger and Holly were still snuggled into the sleeping bag – inside the tent, inside the house! – wondering what they would all do today, when May Days, who was already up and about, poked her head back into the tent.

"Come outside. There's something I want to show you," she said.

Tiger, still wearing her striped tiger-print pyjamas, and Holly, as always, wearing a soft white fur coat, followed May Days out on to the front porch. She pointed to where the wall joined the

roof. It looked as if some roughly made clay bowls had been stuck in the corners. Under the eaves of the main roof were lots more bowl shapes and also one in the top corner of the outside toilet.

"What are they?" asked Tiger.

"Swallow nests," said May Days, smiling. "One of my favourite birds."

"But where are the swallows?" said Tiger, as the nests were empty.

"Swallows come here for the spring and summer," said May Days. "They find their way back to the same place every year, tidy up their old nest, lay their eggs and then raise new chicks. Come on, I'll show you what they look like."

They went back to the kitchen and sat at the table to look up swallows in the wildlife book. The little birds had tails like streamers, black coats and bold white chests.

Tiger read: *Small flocks of swallows gather together and prepare to migrate. They fly over 8,000 kilometres from Africa to the UK, arriving in April.*

"But how can they fly so far when they're so small?" said Tiger, amazed.

"Because they are all together to support each other," said May Days, "and they must be very determined to raise their chicks in the best place."

"But why don't they just stay here all the time?"

"It's far too cold in the winter and there's nothing for them to eat," said May Days, looking out of the window. "They would have left Africa about six weeks ago. I thought they'd be here by now."

May Days had a few jobs to do around the house, so she left Tiger in the kitchen to get dressed. Tiger was thinking about the little birds who worked hard each year to restore their old homes so they could move back into them. Then she started thinking about Willowgate.

"This is very silly," Tiger said to Holly, who pricked up her ears and sat looking

at Tiger with wise eyes. "Why doesn't May Days move into the house properly now all the repairs are done?"

It didn't make sense that they were still sleeping in a tent when there was a big empty house that seemed to be waiting for them.

"Are you thinking what I'm thinking, Holly?" The cat tilted her head to the side as if waiting for Tiger to go on. "Maybe the house isn't as finished as we think it is. We'd better go and find out."

Tiger pulled on her T-shirt and Holly stood

up beside her, ready to investigate.

"We'll have to look around the house as carefully as we did in the garden yesterday, and then maybe we'll be able to see what we're waiting for."

They started with the kitchen, looking up and down and around. This was the only room they had used properly right from the start, so there wasn't much to discover here. Outside the kitchen was a tall, empty hall, with two rooms either side. One was small and empty. The other was much larger and led into the conservatory. All the walls had been plastered smooth and painted white, the cobwebs dusted away. Holly's paws

didn't make a sound, but Tiger's footsteps echoed off the bare floorboards, making the house sound very empty.

"Where's all May Days's furniture and carpets and pictures, Holly?" said Tiger.

In the conservatory, May Days grew tropical flowers in pots, tall and bushy, climbing up supports and across the glass roof. When the flowers bloomed, it was the only colourful room in the house.

"I expect all these flowers grow in Africa too," Tiger said to Holly, thinking of how long May Days had lived in Africa and the things she must have got used to seeing.

With their eyes alert for any movement,

just like they had been in the garden the previous day, they spotted a woodlouse crawling past one of the pots. Tiger crouched down and held out a finger to it. The woodlouse wiggled its antennae and then climbed on.

"It must feel like a huge jungle in here to a woodlouse," said Tiger as the cat gave it a good sniff. Tiger let the woodlouse ripple off her finger and back on to the floor. She decided to keep it company for a while in case it felt lonely.

There was a small pile of loose bricks in the corner of the conservatory that the builders had left, and Tiger stacked them into a little house shape.

"There you are – you can move in," said Tiger to the woodlouse, pushing dry leaves in to make a carpet. "It will be much nicer than living under a pot."

Once the woodlouse had settled into its new home, Tiger and Holly went upstairs. There were four bedrooms and the largest had a fireplace, a sink and a

huge cupboard in the wall. The bedroom opposite was the smallest, but, even so, it was much bigger than Tiger's bedroom at home. There was no furniture up here either.

Tiger thought things over. The chimneys at Willowgate that had once been wonky were now straight, and the plumbing didn't gurgle or thump any more. There had been mushrooms growing around the bath, but now it was scrubbed clean. The only thing that didn't seem finished was the smallest bedroom. Floorboards were up and the electrician was coming later to finish the last bit of wiring.

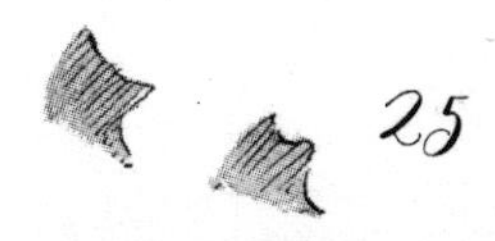

"That must be what it is, Holly. When this room is done, the house will be ready," said Tiger, pleased at what they had discovered by looking carefully.

Tiger and Holly stood in the doorway of the smallest bedroom. The window looked out over the great gardens of Willowgate. The April sunshine streamed in, and Tiger longed to have what May Days had once promised – her own bedroom inside the house.

Tiger skipped down the stairs, with Holly following, excited at the thought that they could soon move into the house properly. Her grandmother was talking on the telephone in the hall. Tiger leaned over the banister, waiting for May Days to finish before she asked if the small room could be hers. But then she heard something that filled her tummy with a horrible feeling.

"We have so much to catch up on. I've missed you terribly, Grace," May Days said into the phone. "I can't wait to see you on Sunday."

Grace lived in Africa and was a dear friend of May Days. They had known each other for years and had worked on the wildlife reserve together. Tiger was returning home on Saturday and then…

Did this mean May Days was planning to go back to live in Africa again? Was that why she had no furniture and was in no hurry to move into the house? And was it why she'd wanted Tiger to see the swallow nests – to show her how the birds had two homes, one here, and one in Africa? Tiger's shoulders sagged and a lump formed in her throat.

"What are we going to do?" Tiger sniffed, clinging to Holly.

Tiger didn't want to talk to May Days about her leaving – it was too hard. She

crept down the last few stairs and tiptoed along the hallway behind May Days, and out through the front door. She needed to think... She had to find a way of making her grandmother want to stay at Willowgate for good.

Chapter 2

Shells

Tiger sat on the lawn cuddling Holly and gazing up at the house. Apart from all the animals that visited and lived in the gardens, Willowgate had been unoccupied for years and years until May Days had bought it. Over the last year, builders, plumbers and all sorts of people had come to help repair the house. But hardly anyone came now it was almost finished, and it suddenly seemed very

quiet and deserted, especially with Tom and Grumps away on holiday. With its wide porch, large windows and long welcoming drive, it looked like it was inviting people in. But the house that Tiger loved now seemed as hollow as an empty shell.

"Poor old house," Tiger whispered in Holly's twitching ear. "It will be all by itself again soon."

Maybe May Days was planning to spend half the time in Africa and half of it at Willowgate, like the swallows? Or worse – much, much worse – what if May Days decided she preferred living in Africa and didn't come back? Tiger hadn't had her grandmother around until she was nine years old, and they had grown close over the last year. Tiger couldn't imagine her life now without May Days in it. But, back in Africa, Grace must miss May Days too. It bothered Tiger terribly that people who were so fond of each other had to live so far apart.

Tiger went back inside the house, trudged up the stairs and into the empty bedroom she wished was hers. Her heart sank as she thought that May Days might never have intended to stay for long. She curled up on the windowsill and, feeling lonely without Tom to talk to, told Holly

her troubles. Holly was a good listener and particularly generous with soft, warm cuddles. But Tiger missed having her friend around. It wasn't that Tom knew all the answers, but he always had good ideas, and it was nice to have someone to rely on and ask for help.

Tiger was distracted from her thoughts by the sound of a vehicle on the gravel drive and looked out of the window. A small blue van had arrived with the name MR SPARK painted on the side in jazzy

white letters. A man got out and walked into the house. Tiger soon heard him speaking to May Days, followed by the stomp of work boots on the bare stairs.

"Hello," said Tiger, when the electrician appeared in the doorway. "Mind the holes," she warned, and he tiptoed carefully across the gaps in the floorboards.

"You must be Tiger," said Mr Spark. "Your grandmother talks about you all the time."

Tiger smiled, even though she was sad inside. One thing she had learned from May Days was that it was better to do something useful than sit around worrying.

"Can I help you?" Tiger said, kneeling carefully on the firm floorboards beside Mr Spark. "I need something to do."

Mr Spark was happy to have an assistant to pass him things from his toolbox. Tiger concentrated on learning what some of the tools were called.

"Hammer, please," Mr Spark said, and used it to lever out a sharp nail. "Can you hold the torch and shine it under there?"

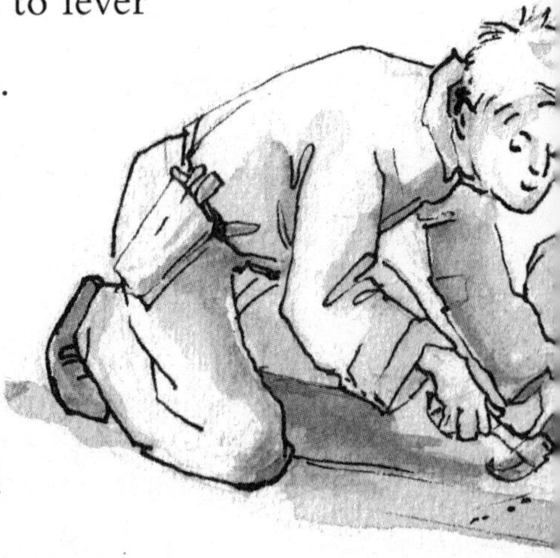

Tiger pointed the torch under

the floorboards so Mr Spark could see where to stretch his arm into the gap to reach for the wires.

"There's something else in there," said Tiger, peering in. "Can you get it for me?"

It was an old newspaper, and Mr Spark gave it to Tiger to have a look at while he joined up some wires.

The newspaper was yellow and it crackled in Tiger's hands. It was dated Thursday 7 May 1953.

"Did people live in the house all those years ago?"

Tiger said, interested that she had found something from the past.

"Lots of people have come and gone from here. The house was built over two hundred years ago," said Mr Spark. "Snippers, please."

Tiger passed the snippers then looked through the newspaper while she waited for her next instruction. She turned a page and couldn't believe her eyes. A headline read MAY DAY FAYRE and there was a photograph of lots of people standing on the lawn of Willowgate House.

"Look!" Tiger said, showing the page to Mr Spark. "Look at all the people who

visited here." She read the article out loud to him.

"More than a hundred people attended the annual May Day Fayre at Willowgate House last Saturday, hosted by Mrs Humble as she celebrated her eightieth birthday. Mrs Humble sat outside on the

porch and watched the sack races and the children maypole dancing." Tiger was amazed and looked up at Mr Spark, who was peering closely at the photo.

"I think that's my dad, Jimmy!" he said, pointing to the face of a boy in the picture.

Mr Spark told Tiger that his dad still lived in the village and ran the post-office store. Everybody stopped by the post office. It was the hub of the village.

"Why don't you and your grandmother go and ask him about it some time? He loves to chat about the old days," said Mr Spark, although he thought that May Days would have already heard from someone in the village about the history of the May Day Fayre at Willowgate House.

Tiger's worries had gone while she'd been helping Mr Spark. But when she looked out of the window and saw May Days outside, staring up at the sky and looking out for the swallows from Africa, the anxious feeling returned.

All afternoon Tiger helped Mr Spark. She enjoyed learning about tools and the electrics, but her mind kept coming back to May Days, and all the things she had before in Africa and all the things she had now at Willowgate. Both places had lots of wildlife. In both places May Days had

lived in a tent. May Days had made good friends in Africa… But with Grumps and Tom away, who were May Days's friends at Willowgate?

Tiger lay in her camp bed that night (still in the tent, in the kitchen) with Holly tucked into the crook of her arm. She was staring at the newspaper when May Days brought her a mug of hot chocolate and got into bed too.

"What's that you've found?" asked May Days.

"A special piece of Willowgate history," said Tiger, showing her the article.

"That was all a very long time ago," said May Days, distracted by a hooting owl outside.

"Can we go and talk to Jimmy about it tomorrow?" said Tiger.

May Days hesitated at first. "Who's Jimmy?"

Tiger thought May Days would know him and was surprised she didn't. She explained that Jimmy was Mr Spark's dad and that he ran the post office.

"Oh, is that his name?" said May Days. "I don't know him very well."

Tiger said she was really interested to find out about the May Day Fayre and that Mr Spark had said that Jimmy was very chatty, so May Days eventually agreed to take her.

Tiger smiled to herself as she went

to sleep. Maybe if May Days made new friends in the village it could help persuade her not to go back to Africa…

Chapter 3

A Spark

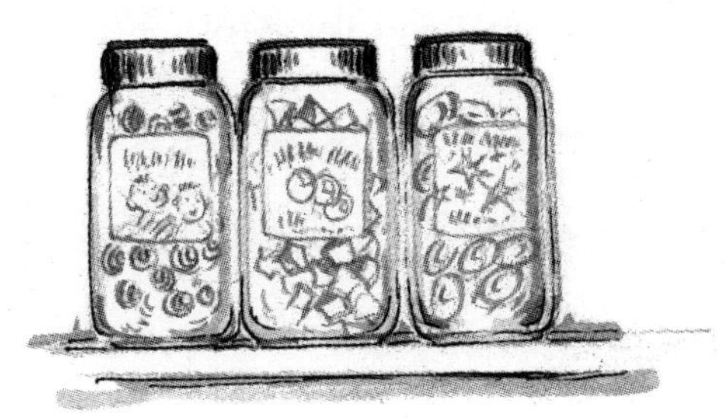

The post-office store was like a shop from a much older time, with posters in the window, a polished wooden floor and shelves crammed with everything from envelopes to tins of beans and jars of sweets. Several people were in the shop and Jimmy Spark was sitting in a small cubicle where you could weigh parcels and buy stamps.

"Good morning, Mrs Days," he said.

"Good morning," she said. They spoke politely for a moment about the weather.

Tiger introduced herself and showed him the photograph in the old newspaper.

"That was the last time we had the annual fayre at Willowgate," said Jimmy. He told them that it had been part of village life since even his parents were young, until Mrs Humble died in the winter of 1953. Other customers overheard and came around the aisles to join in the conversation. May Days greeted them but said little else.

"What was Mrs Humble like?" Tiger asked.

Talk of the wonderful Mrs Humble

bubbled around Tiger, about how she'd organised the fayre around her birthday so that she could invite everyone to come and enjoy her home and garden, and about how she'd loved the wildlife.

"My grandmother has taught me lots about the wildlife, and we've looked after all sorts of animals, even some from the zoo," said Tiger, but when she looked around for May Days to say more, she saw that she was now over by the cereal shelf, reading the side of the packets. May Days must have come to the post office lots of times, but it was as if she didn't know anyone very well at all.

"If you like wildlife, you might be

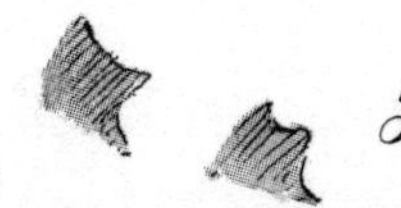

interested to see what's in the cage over there," Jimmy said to Tiger.

On a small table, among the pet food and washing powder, a hamster cage glowed yellow under a warming lamp. There were no hamsters inside. Instead, four pale blue duck eggs lay in a dry grass nest.

"May Days!" said Tiger. "Come and look! One egg is wobbling."

A customer had found the abandoned duck eggs and didn't know what to do with them, so Jimmy had kept them warm for the last week, hoping to save them.

"Can we watch the eggs for a while?"

Tiger asked May Days.

"Time to go – lots of shopping to do," said May Days. Everyone else said goodbye and left the shop, still chatting together about Mrs Humble. Tiger's heart sank. May Days didn't seem to have any friends in the village at all.

"I'd be happy to keep an eye on Tiger while you go shopping, Mrs Days," said Jimmy, saying it would be no trouble at all. Tiger pleaded – she wasn't finished here yet! – and May Days agreed, saying she wouldn't be long.

Tiger sat on a stool at the end of the counter where she could keep an eye on the eggs and talk to Jimmy. Tiger adored

watching the eggs rock, knowing there were fluffy ducklings inside.

"I was hoping to find someone to look after them until they are old enough to look after themselves," Jimmy said.

"I will!" said Tiger.

"Well, you'd better ask Mrs Days first," he said.

"Did you know my grandmother's name is May Days?" Tiger asked.

Jimmy didn't know. He said that May Days had visited the post office before, but she didn't ever stay and chat like everyone else usually did, and always seemed in a hurry. It didn't sound like Tiger's grandmother at all.

Tiger told him how May Days used to live on a wildlife reserve in Africa. She had been busy fixing up Willowgate House and looking after animals, but

she was usually fun and was the most adventurous person Tiger knew.

"She sounds very interesting," Jimmy said, smiling kindly at Tiger.

For the first time, Tiger began to understand something new about her grandmother. May Days was fit and strong, full of passion and courage. She could fix plumbing, climb a ladder to paint the gables and wouldn't bat an eyelid if she came face to face with a rhinoceros. But could it be that she was shy? After all, she had been more used to talking to animals than people. But everyone needed friends – Tiger always looked forward to seeing Tom when she came to stay at Willowgate, and looked forward to seeing her friends from school when she returned home.

Tiger looked down at the newspaper again, at all the people having fun at the fayre, standing in the beautiful gardens at Willowgate. Maybe May Days would be more comfortable making friends in her own home…

"Would people come if we had Willowgate Fayre again?" Tiger said, the spark of an idea beginning to grow. "We'd have to have it on Saturday, though," she said, frowning, remembering May Days was planning to go to Africa on Sunday.

Jimmy thought it was a brilliant idea.

He knew just who to ask for help to make flower arrangements and organise a cake stall, and he even knew somebody who had sacks for a sack race. He stocked bunting and balloons in the store. Tiger wasn't yet sure how they were going to make a maypole. Maybe they could use the washing-line post?

"Would it be in the newspaper again?" Tiger asked, swept away with the excitement of it all.

"Leave it with me. I'll make a telephone call," said Jimmy, laughing. A little more seriously, he said, "Get all your ducklings in a row first. Which means prepare everything step by step, and first

things first: you need to ask Mrs… May Days."

The bell on the shop door rang when May Days returned, saying it really was time to go home now. Tiger needed to ask her grandmother a lot of things –

taking care of the eggs, hosting the fayre and for her to not go back to Africa. She decided to start with the thing that May Days was most likely to agree to.

"I've never seen a duckling being born, and they need someone to look after them until we can find them a home. Can I do it?" she pleaded.

"Yes, that would be fine." May Days smiled. "Tiger is very good at looking after animals," she said to Jimmy. Tiger beamed.

"Good luck with everything," Jimmy said to Tiger, winking. "Perhaps you could stop by for a cup of tea sometime, May?" he said.

"Thank you, Jimmy," May Days said, and blushed.

Already it seemed to Tiger that May Days was beginning to make a new friend.

Tiger decided the best place to keep the duckling eggs warm was in front of the cooking range. But the tent was in the way.

"Can we take the tent down?" she asked May Days. "But please can we still sleep in the kitchen by the duck eggs in case the ducklings are born in the night?"

May Days had been intending to take

the tent down anyway, but only to pitch it outside again so they could sleep under the stars. But she agreed to Tiger's idea as there were a few grey clouds in the sky, which meant it might rain soon.

Tiger put some cardboard on the kitchen floor and covered it with a blanket and put the hamster cage on top of that. For the rest of the afternoon, she lay leaning over the edge of her camp bed watching the eggs with Holly.

"How are the eggs coming along?" asked May Days, later.

One of them had a big crack. Another wobbled a bit. Tiny *peep peeps* came from inside.

"Do you think they are talking to each other or to us?" said Tiger.

"They are egging each other on!" chuckled May Days, and Tiger laughed too. "But it will probably take a while for them to hatch out completely."

After a moment, Tiger decided the time was right for her second question. She took a deep breath and asked May Days if they could hold the fayre again at Willowgate.

"Oh, no, I don't think so. It would be far too much work for me and I wouldn't

know where to start," May Days said.

Tiger was terribly disappointed. She lay awake that night watching the tiny ducklings wriggling and kicking inside their shells, and trying to think of what she could say to convince May Days to say yes to the fayre. If May Days didn't make any new friends, then there'd be nothing to stop her moving back to Africa. Tiger's heart felt heavy again.

Chapter 4

What Are Villages For?

Tiger had to find a way to persuade May Days to hold the fayre at Willowgate. But there was very little time left.

Mr Spark called from upstairs where he was finishing the wiring.

"Tiger! Come and see what I've found."

Glad to be distracted, Tiger bounded up the stairs and into the small bedroom.

Mr Spark showed her an old penny, a pair of spectacles, a small doll with a china face and a photograph, all of which had been hidden under the floorboards.

The photograph was of a lady in a long dress and a little girl leaning against her. On the back, written with a blue-ink pen, were the words "Caroline, aged ten".

Who was Caroline? Had this been her bedroom? Did she know Mrs Humble?

Tiger asked if they could take up some more floorboards to see what else they might find, and she knelt down to point the torch underneath.

"I can see a book!" she said.

Mr Spark gave her a long stick and she poked it under the gap and dragged out the book. It was small, dark green and covered in leather, with a narrow ribbon tied round it. On the front, in gold lettering, was printed: 1883.

"It's a diary!" said Tiger, opening it. She gasped when she found written inside the cover:

This diary belongs to
Caroline Humble, aged ten.
If found, please return to
Willowgate House.

Tiger was holding more history in her hands. She ran down the stairs to find May Days.

"Caroline Humble must have grown up to be Mrs Humble, the same lady who owned Willowgate and held the fayre when she was eighty!" said Tiger, turning the page. Tiger and May Days read the first entry together:

Monday 1st January 1883. Blue sky, frosty and cold.

We went down to the bottom of the garden this morning and saw our first robin of the new year. I'm so happy to be at Willowgate again with my grandmother. We are already planning a drawing competition for the fayre in May.

Nothing else was written, but a beautiful pencil drawing, of a robin amongst frosted ferns, decorated the rest of the page.

"Caroline liked drawing, the same as me!" said Tiger. "And the woman in the photograph next to her must be her grandmother! It's just like you and me, May Days!" She looked longingly at the photograph. "If I live here one day, I'll hold the fayre again," said Tiger, without thinking.

May Days put her arms round Tiger. "Does it really mean that much to you?"

Tiger nodded. "Jimmy said it's what villages are for. That people should help each other and make memories together."

"They say something similar to that in the villages of Africa," said May Days, smiling warmly. "But, if we did host the

fayre, we'd have to do it very soon."

Tiger's heart sank. This must mean she really was leaving.

"How about Saturday? I'm sure people from the village will help," said Tiger in a very small voice, trying not to think about May Days leaving on Sunday. If she could make everything at Willowgate as good as, or even better than, Africa, then maybe May Days would stay?

May Days agreed at last. Tiger was relieved and straight away drew a poster with a picture of Willowgate house on it, and they set off to the post-office store. Tiger couldn't wait to tell Jimmy that the May Day Fayre was back in business!

The bell rang when they walked into the store. Since the last visit, Jimmy had put a small table and some chairs beside the counter. On the table was a teapot and cosy, a flask of milk and a couple of books and magazines.

"It's for anyone who wants to come and sit and chat. Or people might want to leave something on the table that someone else might like," he said.

"You mean it's a table for making friends?" said Tiger, looking up hopefully at her grandmother.

"I always love a chat," said Jimmy,

smiling. "Take a seat, May," he said, offering her a chair.

Jimmy was delighted when they told him about the fayre. He told May Days everything he could remember from the last one. May Days was worried that it was too short notice, but Jimmy laughed and said he was sure people would come. Once they had decided the details, Tiger wrote on the poster:

Everyone is welcome to
a historical event!
The return of the MAY DAY FAYRE
At WILLOWGATE HOUSE
This SATURDAY 2pm – 5pm

Jimmy photocopied the poster and taped one to the shop door and another one in the window. He then placed a stack on the table for people to take and share out. Tiger chose some yellow balloons and colourful ribbons from the shop. Customers came in and were thrilled to hear of the return of the fayre.

"Who lives at Willowgate now?" asked a lady.

"My grandmother," said Tiger, handing her a poster. "Here she is. This is May Days."

The lady smiled and said hello to May Days. She asked her about the work being done on the house, and May Days

replied that Mr Spark had just finished the last bit. There was a short silence before May Days asked if anyone had seen the swallows yet. She seemed much more comfortable talking about the birds. Apparently there were many empty nests around the village, waiting for the return

of the swallows. Tiger hoped May Days would find it very hard to go back to Africa until she'd at least seen the swallows.

This is how things should be, thought Tiger, as she and May Days sat happily together in the kitchen that evening. They were watching over the eggs, when suddenly there was a crackling sound and the first duckling burst out, kicking off its shell. It peeped a few times then flopped over, exhausted.

"Even tiny little ducklings are strong!" Tiger said. "But is it all right?" The duckling was damp and bedraggled, and nothing like the fluffy chick she had expected to see.

"They change like magic," said May Days. "Their downy feathers will dry out in a few hours, you'll see."

Soon, the second egg cracked and part of the shell popped off, wobbling as the duckling pushed and pushed inside. And then the third, and then the fourth, all fighting to come out into the world.

Holly purred constantly as two brown-and-yellow ducklings and two all-yellow

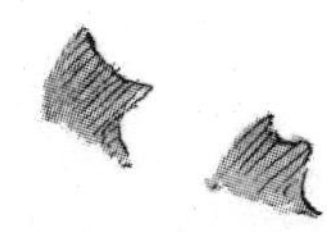

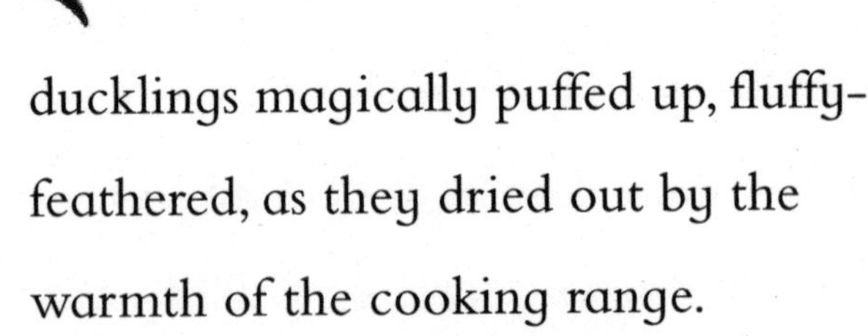

ducklings magically puffed up, fluffy-feathered, as they dried out by the warmth of the cooking range.

Tiger lay awake that night, unable to take her eyes of the ducklings. When at last they fell asleep, huddled in a pile, she picked up Caroline Humble's diary and turned to today's date in 1883 to see what had happened on that day all those years ago.

Wednesday 25th April 1883. Sunny.
I heard my first cuckoo today but didn't see it. Grandma told me they only stay for a few months and then they go back to Africa

in June. The chicks will follow them a few weeks later. There must be something even more amazing in Africa than Willowgate because it's such a long way to fly.

Tiger was again painfully reminded of how May Days loved Africa, and might go back there. She needed to share how she was feeling, and so she wrote in the cover of her new diary which she had bought in the post-office store:

This diary belongs to Tiger Days,
aged nine.
If found, please return to
Willowgate House.

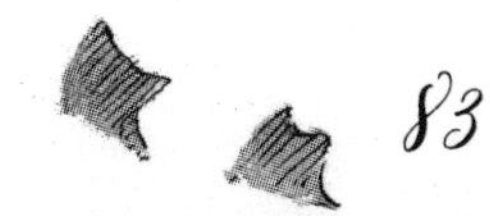

And she began writing and making her own history…

Wednesday 26th April. Sunny. A few clouds. No swallows.

Today four ducklings were born. I love them, and Holly and I are going to look after them. They are the sweetest things I've ever seen. I love my grandmother too and I hope she stays at Willowgate forever, like Caroline Humble did.

Chapter 5

Ducklings In a Row

Thursday 26th April 1883. Blue skies and bubbly white clouds.

Ducklings are on the pond in the garden with the mother duck today. There are eight of them, and they are the sweetest things I have ever seen.

"We wrote exactly the same thing about ducklings!" Tiger said to Holly.

Caroline had also drawn a beautiful picture of a pond and the ducks. Tiger wondered for a moment if the pond was in the village, but the diary definitely said, "in the garden".

"Hmmm," she said to Holly, who was purring at her side. "I wonder where it is."

Reading the diary and looking after the fluffy, sleepy ducklings helped Tiger forget all her worries. The chicks clambered unsteadily over each other, peeping and cheeping, and then gathered again in a heap on the side of the cage next to where Holly and Tiger sat. The cat purred, her paws and tail tucked under, her eyes half closed. But the ducklings needed to strengthen their legs outside the cage, and Tiger worried that a cat couldn't help being a cat.

"Would Holly try to eat them if I let them out?" Tiger asked May Days.

"I've known farm cats to raise baby geese and chickens," said May Days. Tiger wasn't completely surprised, as Holly had once curled up with an orphaned baby warthog and played with fox cubs. "But you'll need to keep a close eye on her at first," said May Days.

Tiger filled a shallow tray with water to let the chicks try it out. Holly sat

beside Tiger as the ducklings stumbled out of the cage and rushed over to them. Holly seemed unsure what to do and stepped away, which only made the ducklings quickly waddle towards her, knocking into the tray and spilling it.

Tiger only looked away for a second to get a cloth, but when she turned back she couldn't see the ducklings anywhere, only Holly licking her whiskers.

"Holly, NO!" said Tiger, panicking, but then she looked again and saw the ducklings had gathered around her own feet. Holly was taking no notice of them at all. Tiger sighed with relief.

The ducklings clambered in and out of the water tray, and back to Tiger's side, shaking their wet, downy feathers while Holly looked on. Tiger picked up a duckling. It was light and warm, and its soft feet padded on her palm. She scooped them all up, put them in her lap and wrapped her arms around them lovingly.

Soon the ducklings were following Tiger everywhere, and Holly followed them too, all in a line. Around the kitchen,

to the conservatory and then to the outside bathroom when Tiger needed to use the loo. The ducklings cheeped outside before wriggling through the gap underneath the door to be with her. They pecked at the loose end of the toilet paper and Tiger grabbed it quickly before they unravelled it all.

They played follow-my-leader around the house until Tiger saw three ladies standing by the front door.

Throughout the day, lots of villagers came to Willowgate to ask how they could help with the fayre. Tiger was so pleased. Even the house felt happy having all these people in it.

After a while, May Days left the front door wide open and the hallway floorboards echoed with the footsteps of people offering things that might be needed. Tiger wrote their names and how they would help on a list in her diary, so she had a record of everything.

May Days kept a teapot topped up and

Tiger added more biscuits to a plate from time to time, saving some crumbs for the ducklings.

Later that afternoon, when all the visitors had gone and May Days was out in the garden somewhere, the doorbell rang once more.

"I've come about the fayre," said the young woman at the door.

"I'm Tiger and this is Holly and our ducklings." She beckoned the woman to join their line to walk down the hall and back to the kitchen.

"Do you normally have ducks living in the house?" asked the woman, smiling.

"We had a warthog living in the kitchen once!" Tiger said.

Tiger poured the woman a cup of tea and offered her a chair at the table. Tiger felt something warm on her feet. Looking down, she saw the ducklings had snuggled up to her again, and the cat was curled around them, keeping them cosy with her fur.

Tiger smiled. "What's your name, please?" she asked the lady.

"Jaya de Silva," the lady replied.

"What would you like to do for the fayre?" asked Tiger.

"Record history," said Jaya.

Tiger looked up, surprised at her answer.

"Jimmy Spark called me," Jaya explained. "I'm a journalist. I'm interested in doing a story about the new Willowgate Fayre and who lives here now."

Tiger thought this was a wonderful idea and showed Jaya the photograph of Caroline Humble, aged ten, with her grandmother.

"They were like me and my grandmother are now," Tiger said. "I hope she stays here for her whole life too."

"Don't you think she will?" said Jaya, as Tiger looked very sad.

Tiger told her how important it was to her to have her grandmother here after all the years they had been apart.

"She sounds very special, just like Mrs Humble," Jaya said. She had brought some photographs of the previous fayres held at Willowgate.

"There's the duck pond!" gasped Tiger, pointing to one of the photographs. "But I've never seen it. Will you help me find it? It would be a perfect home for the ducklings!"

Jaya agreed with a smile, and they headed across the lawn, carrying two ducklings each, followed by the cat.

"It was near a willow tree," Jaya said.

"Down by the gate!" said Tiger.

At first, there was no sign of the old pond. Then Tiger noticed some tall leaves similar to the reeds by the river. This must mean water! Under her feet, she felt lumpy stones, covered in moss. Next to the stones, the ground was muddy and very wet.

"This is it!" said Tiger, testing the soggy ground. "But it's overgrown."

May Days appeared, driving across the lawn on her sit-on mower, cutting the

grass ready for the fayre. "What are you up to?" she said, smiling.

"I've found somewhere for the ducks to live! It's the old pond," said Tiger. A lump came to her throat as she thought of losing May Days, but she carried on,

saying things she hoped would persuade her grandmother to stay. "Also, other

animals might come and drink and swim, and you could watch them here, like you used to in Africa."

"I'd like to hear about your time in Africa," said Jaya, introducing herself. She had lots of questions for May Days and they went back to the house to chat.

Tiger left the ducklings and cat snuggled in her cardigan in the grass. She pulled moss from the stones, following the outline around until she had uncovered an oval-shaped pond, full of mud and weeds. She fetched a spade and started digging until her muscles ached. It was tough work, and with nobody to help finish it Tiger decided she should prepare the ducklings instead, by teaching them how to swim.

With the bath upstairs in the house filled with warmish water, Tiger made a slope with a plank of wood running from the floor up to the rim of the bath, scattering crumbs along it to encourage the ducklings to climb up. They soon got the idea, and waddled up to the top, jostling against each other, unwilling to jump in.

Then Tiger had an idea – she changed into her swimming costume and climbed in the bath first! The ducklings soon leapt off the edge and were bobbing all around her. Tiger rested her feet on the taps so

they could all climb on her legs. They stayed in the bath, practising swimming and climbing in and out, until Tiger was happy they had learned what to do.

Thursday 27th April. Sunny. White clouds. No swallows.

Jaya de Silva (aged 27) is going to write a report in the newspaper about the fayre and is coming back on Saturday with a photographer. We found the old pond by the willow tree. I wish the ducklings could live here. I love Willowgate and May Days and it would never be the same without them.

Chapter 6

In for a Splash

Tiger was in bed with Holly the cat, and the ducklings were in their cage, cocooned in a fluffy heap. Tiger turned to today's date in Caroline's diary.

Friday 27th April 1883. Showers all day. Grandma taught me a rhyme about the weather:

"Oak before ash, we're in for a splash;
Ash before oak, we're in for a soak."

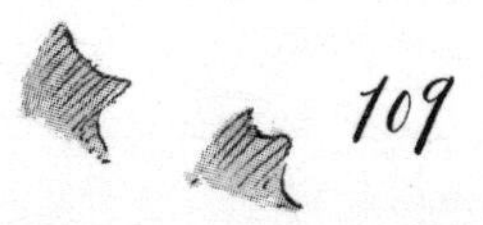

Grandma said that the leaves of the oak trees came out first at Willowgate this year, and that's a good thing because it means we'll only have showers and no downpours this spring. Fingers crossed for no showers at all for the fayre tomorrow!

Tiger heard a van rattling up the drive. She quickly dressed and raced out the door to see if it had anything to do with the fayre.

"Delivery for Willowgate," said the man, checking his paperwork.

"What is it?" asked Tiger.

"Furniture," he said. Tiger gasped. Did this mean May Days really was going to move into the house at last?

"I forgot I had all these things," said May Days, coming out. "I've had it in storage since I came back from Africa."

"Where would you like it?" asked the man, opening the back of the van. "Do you want some help unpacking?"

"Oh, we've got the fayre on Saturday, and then Sunday . . ." May Days muttered to herself. "No, thank you. If you could just stack everything in the big room and we'll leave it there."

Tiger's heart sank again. The empty house was more like a storeroom than a home! And May Days seemed to have no intention of moving in properly.

Downhearted, Tiger decided to keep busy, so when the van had gone she persuaded May Days to come down the garden to help her finish digging out the pond. They worked hard to clear the weeds and overgrown reeds, digging out some of the mud to make a bank and slope. They were both very quiet, not speaking about the things that they probably should have been, and then May Days went back up to the house. Tiger unreeled the hose and began to fill the pond back up with water, to make a home for the ducklings. Her heart felt as if it had dropped down a deep hole. But she wasn't going to give up trying to convince May Days to stay.

And then an idea occurred to her – maybe if she put some of the furniture where it belonged then her grandmother might see how homely Willowgate could be and decide to stay.

Running back to the house, Tiger got to work immediately, unpacking the boxes, opening lids and unravelling bubble wrap and newspaper. There were patterned woven baskets of all sizes, carved masks decorated with beads, paintings and rugs and many, many wooden figures of African animals. Tiger had her arms full when she heard a floorboard creak and the peep of the ducklings and turned round to see May Days peering through the door, the ducklings spilling into the room and rushing over to Tiger.

"Leave that for now," said May Days, coming into the room and pulling the wrapping from a wicker chair. She sat down and invited Tiger on to her lap as the ducklings investigated the wrapping on the floor and pecked at pieces of string.

"It's so nice to see all my things again," said May Days.

Tiger lifted up the items she was holding – a woven basket and a wooden mask. May Days described how she had learned to weave baskets, though nothing as complicated as the layers of colour in the little round basket that Tiger held. They stared at a wooden mask with a strong face, studded with bright coloured beads.

"What is the mask for?" asked Tiger.

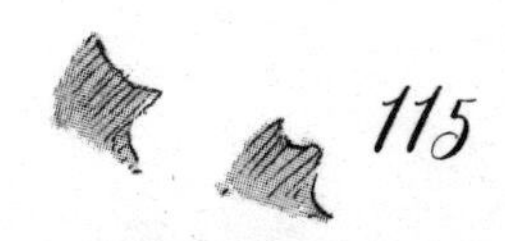

"It was to wear in dancing ceremonies. Mr Kamanga gave it to me. He was Grace's father," said May Days as Tiger leaned back against her grandmother's shoulder. "He said it reminded him of me!" which made Tiger laugh. "Mr Kamanga helped get us permission to have the land for the wildlife reserve. I gave him my watch to thank him, as he was always very late," May Days chuckled. "Which reminds me, I ought to give Grace a call, make sure I've got the flight time right for Sunday."

Mays Days helped Tiger off her lap and walked out of the room and Tiger felt her throat tighten. Why hadn't May Days talked to her about leaving? Why was she acting like it didn't matter? Would she miss Tiger at all?

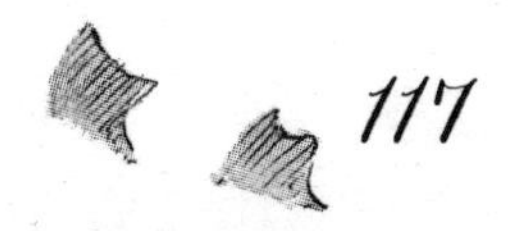

Tiger looked down at the ducklings now cheeping around her feet. They needed her to look after them, just like she needed May Days, even if she didn't realise it. Tiger made the ducklings a portable nest out of May Days's shallow, colourful African basket, which had handles so she could carry the ducklings with her and they wouldn't get worn out. There was brightness and colour everywhere around her but only sadness in Tiger's heart. Willowgate was only just beginning to look and feel like a home, but it was also like a nest that would soon be abandoned.

That evening there was still no sign of the swallows between the clouds bowling across the sky. Everything kept reminding Tiger of what it would be like without her grandmother. She wrote all her feelings in her diary.

Friday 28th April. Cloudy. No swallows.

May Days helped me dig the pond. It took all afternoon to fill it up with water. I have to leave it overnight to see if it stays full. If it doesn't, there might be a hole in the bottom. I'm trying to think of

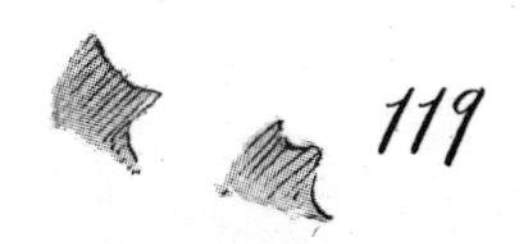

names for the ducklings, but I can't because I'm so worried about what will happen to them when May Days goes. All my happiness keeps leaking out.

And then it all hurt too much.

"Please, Dad," Tiger pleaded, when she phoned home, "there are only four ducklings, and only one cat. Can I bring them home? When the ducklings are old enough, I can take them down to the park and they can live on the pond there."

"Willowgate is a much better place for them all to live," Mr Days said, trying not to sound too panicked about having a miniature zoo in their very small back garden.

"But May Days will be going on Sunday, and nobody will be here to look after them."

"Where's May Days going?" he said, sounding surprised.

"She's moving back to Africa."

The line went quiet for a moment and then he said, "Go and get May Days. I need to speak to her."

"Tell her we all need her to stay here," said Tiger, her voice wobbling.

May Days came to the phone and listened to her son talk for a long time. Tiger stood by, watching May

Days, hoping to hear or see something that would tell her that May Days had changed her mind. When she eventually got off the phone, May Days turned to see Tiger watching her sadly. Immediately she gathered her granddaughter into her arms.

"I think we've got our wires crossed," May Days said kindly. "What makes you think I'm going back to Africa?"

"You're not?" said Tiger hopefully. "But I heard you tell Grace you would see her on Sunday!"

May Days chuckled. "That's because Grace is coming here! Grace is going to help me –" May Days hesitated for a moment before going on – "choose new beds and curtains, now the house is finished." She smiled. "Would you like to meet her?"

That night, Tiger added a couple more lines to her diary.

Friday 28th April. It's night-time but it feels sunny and glorious!

My grandmother isn't going back to

Africa! Dad said I can stay until late on Sunday and go with May Days to the airport to pick up Grace. I am so happy. Africa is coming here! The ducklings have a home and I can see May Days, Holly, Tom and Grumps whenever I come to stay. I can't wait for the fayre tomorrow!

Chapter 7

In For a Soak

Everything had been organised for the fayre. But nobody had planned for the torrential rain that poured down on Saturday morning. Tiger asked May Days if she had noticed whether the leaves on the ash or the oak had come out first that year.

"It was the ash," said May Days. "I remember seeing it."

"Ash before oak, we're in for a soak!"

said Tiger. She went to all the windows of the house, staring at the sky, hoping she would see a break in the clouds. She was worried that if it kept raining nobody would come to the fayre.

Tiger read Caroline Humble's diary to see what she had written on the day of the first fayre.

Saturday 28th April, 1883. Sunshine and blue skies.

We had practised our maypole dance at school and everyone enjoyed it, even Jimmy Spark who got tangled up in the ribbons. Henry Thomas won the sack race. Mrs Bridges won the cake competition because her fruit cake tasted mostly of sherry. Grandma sat with her friends on the porch and watched everyone enjoying themselves. One day, I hope I'll be like her.

Caroline Humble hadn't drawn any pictures of the fayre in 1883, but she had glued in a photograph of her and her grandmother feeding the ducks in the pond, with the maypole in the background.

Tiger lifted up her ducklings in their African nest-basket so they could look out of the window with her. The leaves on the trees drooped, puddles gathered on the patio and the pond splashed upwards

with the hard rain. It didn't look as if it was going to stop. Tiger sighed deeply.

Everybody had worked hard for the fayre. It would have been so nice to have all their new friends visit Willowgate. And then she saw a tall person and a small person wearing very long raincoats, with the hoods over their heads, jogging up the drive, waving.

"May Days!" Tiger called as she ran to the front door to greet them. "Tom and Grumps are back from their holiday!"

"We came back from the seaside last night because it started to rain," Tom explained as he stood dripping in the hallway. "We saw the posters for the fayre in the village and have come to see if we can help."

"Nobody can help change the weather," said Tiger, putting on a brave smile. She was so pleased to see Tom and

overjoyed that May Days wasn't leaving, but she was still disappointed that the fayre wasn't going to take place.

"It's nice weather for ducks but nobody else," said Grumps, and they all agreed that they wouldn't be able to set up the stalls or put up bunting in the rain, even if anyone did come.

"I'd better go into the village and let everyone know the fayre is cancelled," said May Days, who was just as disappointed as Tiger.

"We'll all come with you," said Grumps. May Days thanked him, but insisted he and Tom dry out by the cooking range first.

Tom's eager eyes were drawn to the fluffy bundle in the basket. Tiger gave him the ducklings to hold, one at a time.

Tom had lots to tell Tiger about boats and sandcastles on holiday. And Tiger had lots to tell Tom about ducklings and history, showing him Caroline's diary and the old newspaper article from 1953.

"Henry Thomas won the sack race?" Tom said, wide-eyed as he read the dairy. He looked at the photograph in the newspaper. "That's Grumps! Grumps is Henry Thomas!" he said. "He's got some old photographs of the village from when he was a boy too."

Tiger thought about Grumps growing up in the village and how everyone who lived there shared a history, like May Days with her friends in Africa. The fayre was meant to bring people together, to make new memories, and maybe that could still happen...

"Don't cancel the fayre, May Days!" said Tiger, rushing after her. "I've got an idea!"

Tiger's idea was a brilliant one and the fayre did go ahead. Tiger decided to record the day in her diary so that it would never be forgotten…

Saturday 29th April. Rain, rain and more rain – nice weather for ducks!

Everyone came inside Willowgate House for May Days's historical fayre. Tom and I put the bunting around the walls in each room downstairs and made two "history rooms". In the sitting room we created the May Days History Room. We put out all May Days's

things from Africa. I liked the tall carving of the antelope with spirally horns best. It was polished silky smooth. We had a table with lots of beads so that people could make an African bracelet.

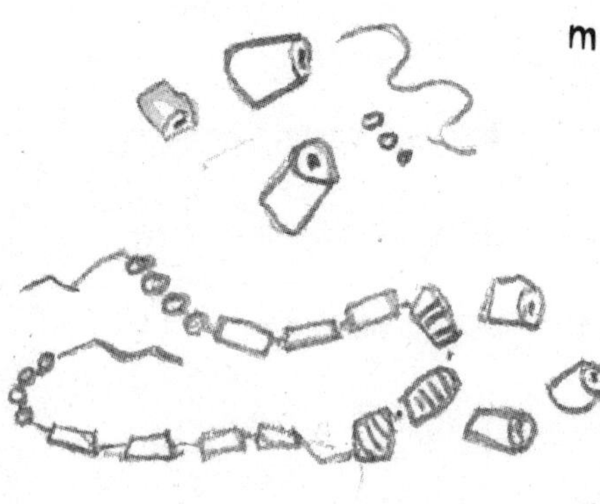

Everyone wanted to ask May Days about her time on the wildlife reserve. I'm so proud of what my grandmother has done in her life. Jaya wrote lots of things down and the photographer took lots of pictures.

In the other room, we made the Willowgate Village History Room, where we put all the old things Mr Spark found under the floorboards, Jaya's old newspaper cuttings and Grumps's old photographs. Jimmy Spark and Grumps have been friends ever since school and all the older people shared stories about the good old days. Jimmy and Grumps had a sack race up the hall. Grumps won again.

Lots of people brought cakes and a man and a lady from the village boiled the kettle for cups of tea about a hundred times. We ate

nearly all the cakes and nobody could decide on a winner because they were all delicious.

We couldn't do the maypole dancing, but it didn't matter. The children from the village didn't know how to do it any more anyway. The teacher from the school said she'd find out and teach them, ready for next year. (Next year!)

All the children wanted to hold the ducklings and I made sure everyone was gentle. I tied ribbons to yellow balloons and we all drew a picture of a duckling on them and then blew them up, so everyone had their own duckling. We all made a line and I showed everyone around the house, with the real ducklings and balloon ducklings following us.

We found Holly in the kitchen, curled up on Mrs Cox's lap. Lots of people already knew Holly because

she is friendly and likes to go wandering around other people's houses.

I showed people the house I'd made for the woodlouse in the conservatory and we found that about ten woodlice had moved in now (they are hard to count because they keep wriggling).

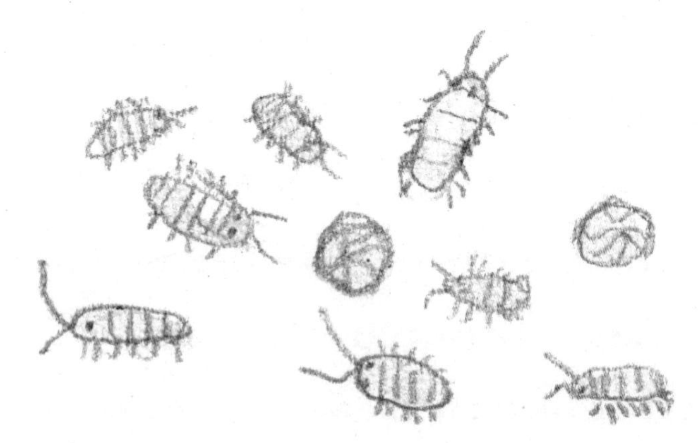

I made a competition for people to choose names for the ducklings. They had to write a name on a piece of paper and the reason why they'd chosen it. Tom helped me decide the winning names. The two yellow ones are now called Caroline and April (April was Caroline Humble's grandmother's name). The two brown-and-yellow ones are called Henry and James, after Grumps and Jimmy Spark. I forgot all about prizes. Instead, I wrote a certificate for the winners and said they could have a wildlife tour with me and Tom when we come

back to Willowgate in the summer.

Right at the end of the fayre, it finally stopped raining. The sun came out and May Days asked everyone to come outside, but to be quiet.

All along the telephone wire and swooping over the house were lots of brave little swallows. They had flown all the way from Africa and come home to Willowgate.

And then, when everyone had gone home, Tiger and Tom went upstairs to the smallest bedroom and hid some interesting things under the floorboards.

Hopefully, one day, someone else will find them…

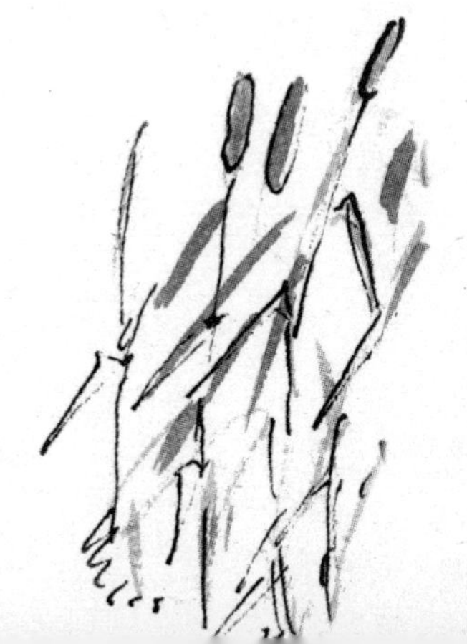

Chapter 8

Here to Stay

Early on Sunday morning, Tiger read Caroline Humble's diary:

Sunday 29 April 1883. Cloudy and grey.

Surprise! Grandma and I saw the swallows come back. It was so lovely to see them all again.

Caroline had drawn tiny little birds across the pages.

Tiger carried her ducklings outside in their basket and looked up at the swallows flitting between the eaves of the house and the sky, filling the air with their twittering. She walked across the lawn to check if the pond had stayed full. Tiger had thought that history was all about a time when things were different. But there were many things that were the same today as all those years ago. The swallows arrived on almost the same day! Tiger and Caroline both liked to draw. Caroline and her grandmother loved the wildlife and each other, the same as Tiger and May Days did. And the pond was still full of water.

Tiger and May Days drove to the airport. The ducklings went with them in their basket as it was nearly time for Tiger to go home and she wanted to spend every last minute she could with them.

At the airport arrival gate they waited, watching the crowds coming through with their suitcases, Tiger asking every few seconds, "Is that Grace?" And then at last Tiger knew Grace had arrived when a voice sang across the hall, "May Days! May Days!"

"Grace! You're here at last!" May Days called back, and they ran to greet each other.

"I'm Tiger," said Tiger, wanting to be part of their friendship too.

"We have lions and cheetahs and leopards in Africa, but you are my first Tiger," Grace said, touching Tiger's cheek, which glowed happily.

Tiger thought Grace was lovely with her braided hair, big smile and soft, melodic voice. She would be staying with May Days for quite a few weeks and Tiger wished she could stay at Willowgate longer and talk about animals forever more with them both.

"Depending on how things go, I might still be here when you next visit," said Grace.

"Oh, do you think it will take a long time to find the right curtains?" asked Tiger.

Grace looked a bit confused. "Well as you know, we will be spending time—" She stopped talking, frowning a little at May Days, who had a finger to her lips. "Have you not told Tiger?" Grace said.

"As she was supposed to be going home yesterday, I thought it would be better to leave it as a surprise for next

time she visits," May Days explained.

"What surprise?" said Tiger.

"A BIG surprise!" laughed Grace and May Days together.

Tiger was fit to burst with excitement as she noticed they weren't heading back to Willowgate but had turned off the main road where a sign pointed to the zoo.

"One day, I'd like to take you out to Africa and show you all the wonderful things there," said May Days. "But, occasionally, things are not so good for some animals, especially when there are very few left of their kind."

"Like Wilfred the rhinoceros you both looked after?" said Tiger, knowing that he was rare and endangered, and that May Days had rescued him, and Grace had taken over looking after him when May Days had left Africa. Grace and May Days were both nodding, smiling, tears in their eyes.

"You're so clever, Tiger! Yes, Wilfred is here!" said May Days.

"*Wilfred?*" said Tiger. Of all the animals Tiger wanted to meet, it was the one that her grandmother had loved the best: Wilfred the great big stomping rhinoceros.

"Do you think the ducklings will be scared of him?" she said.

"Not if you're with them," May Days laughed.

They didn't drive through the main entrance, but instead went down a back lane where they met Dennis the zookeeper, who let them into the part of the zoo where visitors couldn't normally go.

Inside a huge building, Tiger, the ducklings, May Days, Grace and Dennis all lined up behind iron bars as thick as tree trunks. Tiger trembled, even though she couldn't see Wilfred yet.

"He's round the corner," said Dennis. "He had a long journey here yesterday and is still getting used to his surroundings. But he'll be safer here in the long run."

"Do you think he'll remember me?" said May Days, and Grace nodded. "You are kind of unforgettable," said Tiger, smiling up at her grandmother.

"Come, come!" May Days called. "Come, come, Wilfred!"

A breathy snort came from the other end of the building, sending a shiver down Tiger's back. "I can hear him," she whispered as Wilfred grunted again.

May Days called once more.

There was a shuffle and the unmistakable sound of something big and heavy trotting towards them. Tiger gasped as the huge, powerful rhinoceros came over, his small ears twitching forward as he

recognised May Days's voice.

May Days's eyes were shining brightly and she squeezed Tiger's hand. There was only one other occasion when Tiger had seen her grandmother look so happy, and that was each time Tiger arrived at Willowgate to stay with her.

"Poor Wilfred," said May Days. "He's had a tough time and he's such a soft old thing."

"Hello, Wilfred," said Tiger, laughing breathlessly. She'd never seen an animal so big so close up in all her life. He looked more like a mountain than something soft, though!

May Days had once told Tiger that Wilfred had become beautiful to her because she had cared for him. Grace put her arm round May Days and they both shared a smile, thinking about everything they had done together to save him. Still holding Tiger's hand, May Days reached out and they both touched Wilfred's thick, rough skin. It made Tiger's heart feel as if it was about to burst.

Tiger looked down at the ducklings, small and soft and fluffy, their tiny heads peeking over the top of the basket to look at the giant armoured creature. May Days was right – they were all so very beautiful when you cared so much.

"I think I want to go and live in Africa for a while when I grow up," said Tiger to Wilfred.

Back at Willowgate House that evening, Tiger eventually handed over the basket of ducklings to May Days, with lots of instructions about how to look after them.

"Caroline likes to go first in the line, and sometimes April gets a little bit left behind because she's smaller than the others," said Tiger. "Holly will help," she said, giving the cat a last cuddle. "Also, you might have to have a bath with

them until they're ready for the pond."

"Sounds like fun," said May Days, chuckling. "Ducklings grow quickly and they will look very different when you come back next time, but I'm sure they will recognise you."

May Days had something she wanted to give Tiger. The photographer had taken a picture of May Days and Tiger at the fayre, and had given her two copies. May Days put one on the mantelpiece above the fireplace. She gave Tiger the other copy.

"It feels like I have two homes now," said Tiger.

"And are you ready to go to your

other home?" said Tiger's dad with a smile. He'd been waiting with the car door open for ages.

"I forgot to show you the swallows!" said Tiger, pulling him back to the porch. "Look, here they come, carrying some mud in their beaks to repair their nests," she said as the little dark feathered birds with their bold white chests swooped in over their heads.

At last, waving out of the car window to her grandmother and Grace, Tiger set off home with her dad. At the bottom of the drive, the car stopped so Tiger could get out and open the gate. She took one last look at the pond she had prepared for Caroline, April, Henry and James.

Already some ducks had made a home there, which meant her ducklings would have plenty of friends in the future.

Tiger couldn't wait to come back in the summer and see how they were all getting on.

Read an extract from Tiger Days's first adventure at Willowgate House.

Tiger Days didn't know anyone who loved tigers as much as she did.

She wore tiger pajamas, socks and slippers, and spent a lot of time in her bedroom reading about tigers and drawing tiger pictures. Her parents would often suggest bike rides and trips to the swimming pool on Saturday afternoons, but Tiger would much rather be in her bedroom doing tiger things.

One Saturday afternoon, her parents appeared at her door.

"You'll never guess who that was on the phone..." said Mom.

"Hmmmm?" said Tiger, not really listening.

Dad rolled his eyes as Tiger's nose stayed firmly buried in her wildlife book. "It was May Days!" he said.

Tiger looked up, surprised. May Days was her grandmother and had been living in Africa on a wildlife reserve since Tiger was a baby.

Whenever May Days phoned, Tiger asked when she was coming to visit, but May Days said it was hard to know because the giraffes or rhinos always needed her more.

This time, May Days had phoned with wonderful news. She had finally come back to England and bought a place called Willowgate House.

"She wants you to go and stay," said Dad. "You can have your first adventure together at the new house."

Tiger wrinkled her nose. She was sometimes nervous about doing new things and the idea of a real-life adventure with May Days was a little scary. She had a feeling May Days wasn't going to be like everyone else's grandmother.

"Won't you be worried about me?" she asked her parents.

"While you're with May Days? Not even for a second," said Mom, although it was obvious that *somebody* was worried.

But Tiger put on a brave smile for her

parents. An adventure with May Days
would be great, wouldn't it?

"Are you sure this is the right house?" said
Tiger.

She stood close to her dad by the gate,
beneath a large drooping willow tree.

Willowgate House was unexpectedly
huge, and it stood at the end of a long
driveway. It had wide windows and tall
chimney pots, and a greenhouse that
leaned slightly to the left.

Tiger tilted her head to the side to see if
it looked any straighter. But it didn't. The
lopsided building made her feel wobbly.

Tiger waited on the doorstep behind Dad while he pulled the bell on the wall beside the door.

The next surprise was May Days.

Weren't grandmothers supposed to be old and gray and worn?

Instead she had curls that were wild and alive. Her sleeves were pushed up, as if she'd done a hard day's work, and she bounded out like the kind of person who didn't sit down very often.

"You're here, at last!" May Days beamed, throwing her arms around Dad first, and then around Tiger. Tiger peered behind her grandmother at the bare floorboards and curved staircase in

the hall. It looked as if nobody had lived here for a very long time.

"You were no bigger than a koala the last time I saw you," May Days said, holding Tiger by the cheeks. Tiger blinked in surprise, and her tummy did a flip.

"You've got a big house," said Tiger, not sure what else to say.

"Too big for one person," May Days said, chuckling like a barrel full of chickens. "Come in! Come in!"

This time at Willowgate House Tiger discovers a mysterious tunnel that has appeared under the shed and someone – or something – has been burying eggs in the garden…

Tiger and her friend Tom decide to become detectives – determined to crack the case!

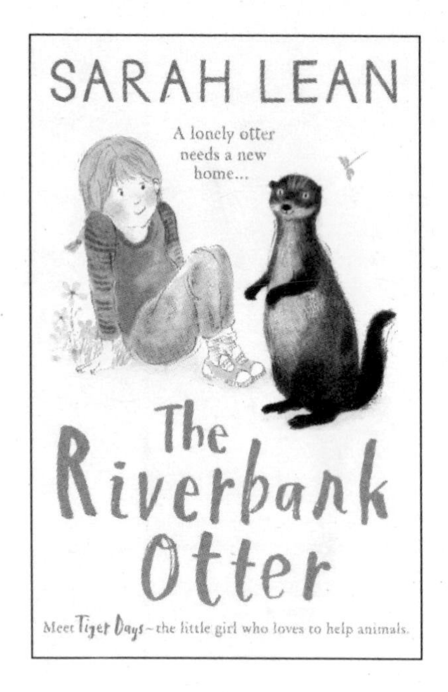

Tiger meets Lucky – an injured otter who can't survive by himself. Tiger has important jobs to do: feeding and caring for Lucky, and also exploring the riverbank in search of the perfect place for him to live. She desperately wants Lucky to get better, but saying goodbye to her new friend won't be easy…